For my gramma Elaine . . .
who always helped me shine

• Little, Brown and Company • Hachette Book Group • 237 Park Avenue, New York, NY 10017 • Visit our
website at lb-kids.com • Little, Brown and Company is a division of Hachette Book Group, Inc. The Little, Brown name and
logo are trademarks of Hachette Book Group, Inc. • The publisher is not responsible for websites (or their content) that are
not owned by the publisher. • First Edition: January 2015 • Library of Congress Cataloging-in-Publication Data • Doerrfeld,
Cori, author, illustrator. • Matilda in the middle / by Cori Doerrfeld. — First edition. • pages cm • Summary: "Matilda is a
bunny who lives with her mom, dad, and many, many siblings. Because she's the middle bunny, she always feels overlooked.
Then one day, her mother enrolls Matilda in dance class, and she falls in love with ballet"— Provided by publisher. •
ISBN 978-0-316-20713-3 • [1. Middle-born children—Fiction. 2. Ballet dancing—Fiction. 3. Rabbits—Fiction.] I. Title. • PZ7.
D6934Mat 2014 • [E]—dc23 • 2013009001 • 10 9 8 7 6 5 4 3 2 1 • SC • Printed in China

A BUNNY BALLET STORY

Matilda
in the Middle

by Cori Doerrfeld

LITTLE, BROWN AND COMPANY
NEW YORK BOSTON

Matilda was a little bunny who lived in a cozy burrow with her mother, her father . . .

. . . and her brothers and sisters—her many, many brothers and sisters.

It was difficult having so many older brothers
and sisters. They were always so busy! They
never had any time to play with Matilda.

Having so many little brothers and sisters
wasn't easy, either. They always got in
the way of everything—and everyone . . .
especially Matilda.

Sometimes, Matilda wondered if she
would always feel lost in the middle.

To her surprise, one morning Matilda's mother said, "I wanted to do something just for you, so I signed you up for bunny ballet. I have a feeling you will be a wonderful ballerina."

(Matilda's mother always seemed to have a feeling about things.)

On her first day of ballet class, Matilda was a little nervous.
But then she saw how beautifully all the other bunnies danced . . .
especially her instructor, Miss Milieu. Step by step,
Matilda was determined to follow along.

Back home, Matilda tried to practice whenever
she could. But her older brothers and sisters never
had time to watch. And her younger brothers and
sisters were in the way more than ever!

Still, each day, in every way, Matilda practiced
ballet in the middle of it all.

Matilda's hard work did not go unnoticed. When Miss Milieu announced the year-end recital, she smiled at Matilda and said, "Matilda, my dear, I want you to dance in the middle of the stage, where everyone can see you!"

"Everyone?!"

Matilda could not wait to tell her family.

At first, Matilda was excited to share her news.
Finally it would be her turn to shine!

But before she knew it, Matilda was back to feeling
lost in the middle . . . just like always.

When the big day arrived, Matilda woke up
still eager to practice her steps. All day long,
she leaped and twirled, waiting for someone to
mention the recital. But Matilda's family was *so*
busy and *so* bothersome that eventually . . .

. . . Matilda did not feel like dancing
at all. In fact, she simply wanted
to be alone.

Most of the time, being alone in such a big, busy family was nearly impossible.

But that afternoon, the burrow grew so silent and still that Matilda could not help but wonder where everybody was.

"SURPRISE!" they all cheered.

Matilda could hardly believe her eyes.

Everyone in her family, from the youngest to the oldest, was there
to make sure that today Matilda was the center of attention.

That evening, Matilda took the stage looking, feeling, and dancing her best. What meant the most to her, however, was knowing that being in the middle . . .

. . . was exactly where she belonged.

ABOUT THE BOOK

This book was edited by Connie Hsu and designed by Saho Fujii. The production manager was Erika Schwartz, and the production editor was Wendy Dopkin.

The illustrations were drawn in pencil on Bristol and inked on watercolor paper. The colors and textures were added digitally with Adobe Photoshop. The text was set in Sackers Antique Roman, and the display types are Dulce and Sackers Antique Roman.